Click,
Clack,
Ho!
Ho!
Ho!

For Mrs. Cooper
—D. C.

For Gracie and Johnny and new little Dan;
for Claire Rose, and Gabby, who is part of the clan;
for Logan and Aidan and Ellis D, too—
Merry Christmas to each and all of you!
—B. L.

ATHENEUM BOOKS FOR YOUNG READERS · An imprint of Simon & Schuster Children's Publishing Division · 1230 Avenue of the Americas, New York, New York 10020 · Text copyright © 2015 by Doreen Cronin · Illustrations copyright © 2015 by Betsy Lewin · All rights reserved, including the right of reproduction in whole or in part in any form. · ATHENEUM BOOKS FOR YOUNG READERS is a registered trademark of Simon & Schuster, Inc. · Atheneum logo is a trademark of Simon & Schuster, Inc. · For information about special discounts for bulk purchases, please contact Simon & Schuster Special Sales at 1-866-506-1949 or business@simonandschuster.com. · The Simon & Schuster Speakers Bureau can bring authors to your live event. For more information or to book an event, contact the Simon & Schuster Speakers Bureau at 1-866-248-3049 or visit our website at www.simonspeakers.com. · Book design by Ann Bobco · The text for this book is set in Filosofia. · The illustrations for this book are rendered in watercolor. · Manufactured in China · 0315 SCP · First Edition · 10 9 8 7 6 5 4 3 2 1 · Library of Congress Cataloging-in-Publication Data · Cronin, Doreen, author. · Click, clack, ho! Ho! Ho! / Doreen Cronin ; illustrated by Betsy Lewin. — First edition. · pages cm · Summary: As Farmer Brown prepares the house for Christmas, Duck tries to play Santa—but he gets stuck in the chimney, along with all the other animals who try to help. · ISBN 978-1-4424-9673-6 (hardcover) · ISBN 978-1-4424-9674-3 (eBook) · 1. Ducks—Juvenile fiction. 2. Animals—Juvenile fiction. 3. Santa Claus—Juvenile fiction. 4. Christmas stories. [1. Ducks—Fiction. 2. Domestic animals—Fiction. 3. Santa Claus—Fiction. 4. Christmas—Fiction.] I. Lewin, Betsy, illustrator. II. Title. · PZ7.C88135Cjo 2015 · [E]—dc23 · 2014043594 · ISBN 978-1-4814-6017-0 (Scholastic edition)

Click, Clack, Ho! Ho! Ho!

Doreen Cronin · Illustrated by Betsy Lewin

Atheneum Books for Young Readers
New York London Toronto Sydney New Delhi

Snow is falling.
Lights twinkle.
A few creatures are stirring.
It is Christmas Eve.

There is a jingle in the air.
Farmer Brown stops to listen.

Santa is on his way.

There is swooshing up above.

Farmer Brown runs to the window.

Santa is getting close.

There is a pitter-patter
on the roof.

Farmer Brown hurries
off to bed.

Santa is almost here!

HO!

HO!

Uh-oh.

Duck is stuck.

The sheep go up
to unstuck Duck.

HO!

HO!

Uh-oh.

The sheep are stuck.

The cows go up
to unstuck Duck.

HO!

HO!

Uh-oh.

The cows are stuck.

The pigs go up to unstuck Duck.

HO!

HO!

Uh-oh.

The pigs are stuck.

They all go up to unstuck Duck.

HO! HO! Uh-oh.
Everyone is stuck!

It is Santa's turn
to unstuck Duck.

HO! HO!

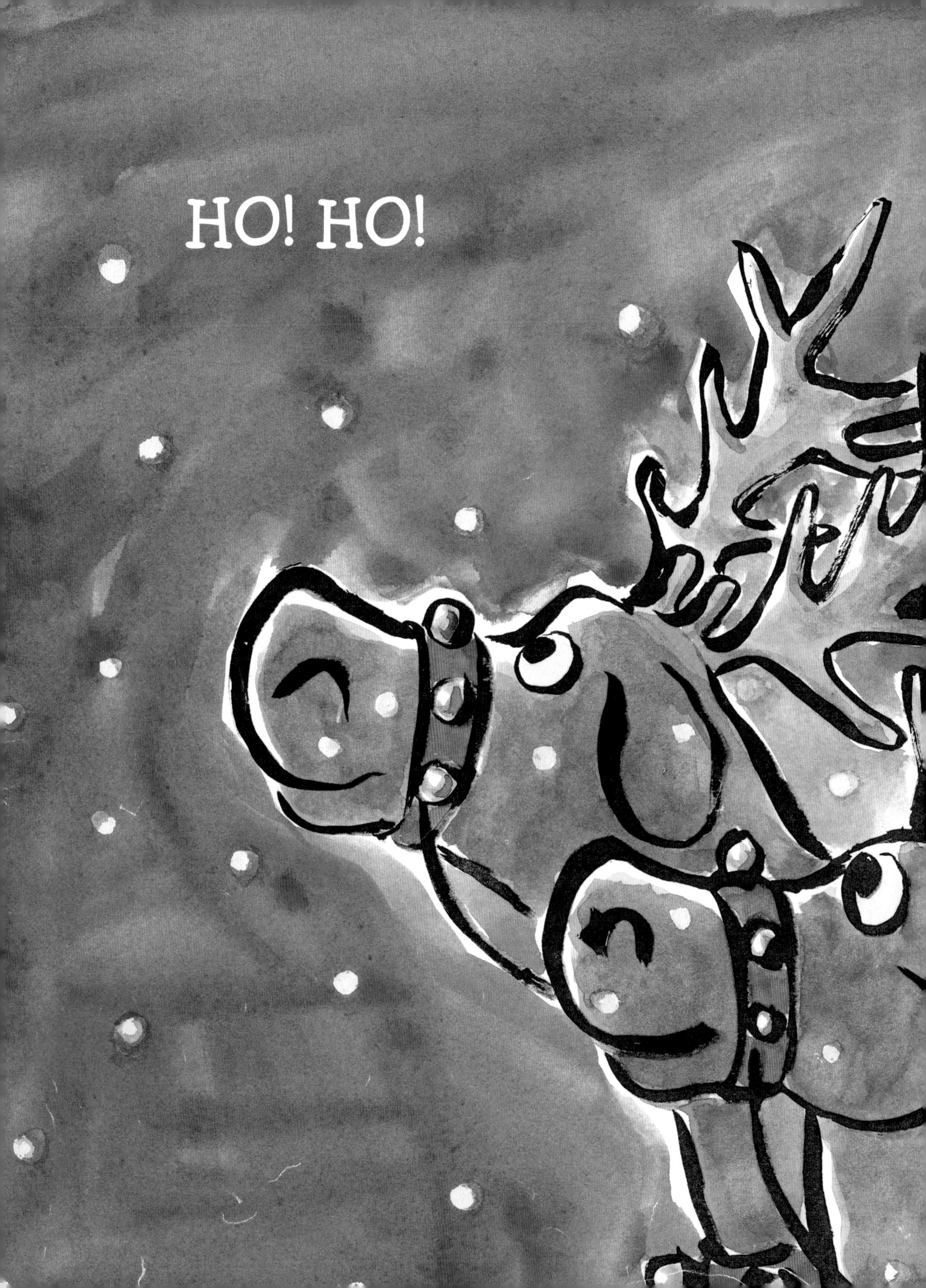

Don't be silly.
Santa would never get stuck!

Now, all around the tree,
in the lights' warm glow . . .

all the creatures are stirring!